Published by Familius LLC, www.familius.com

1254 Commerce Way, Sanger, CA 93657

Familius books are available at special discounts for bulk purchases, whether for sales

promotions or for family or corporate use. For more information, contact Familius Sales at

559-876-2170 or email orders@familius.com.

Library of Congress Control Number: 2019956716

Print ISBN 9781641702416

Ebook ISBN 9781641702980

Printed in China

Edited by Hannah Vinchur and Brooke Jorden

Cover and book design by Carlos Guerrero

10 9 8 7 6 5 4 3 2 1

First Edition

OVER IN THE WOODLAND

A MYTHOLOGICAL COUNTING JOURNEY

WRITTEN BY Nicole and Shar Abreu
ILLUSTRATED BY Susanna Covelli

Can you find the hidden griffin on each page?

Over in the Woodland,
where the mythic creatures roam,

Lived a noble griffin pride
to protect the Woodland home.

"Guard," said the mother.
"We guard every home."

So her young griffins flew
where the mythic creatures roam.

Over in the Woodland, in the glimmer of the sun,
Lived a bright father phoenix and his little phoenix one.

"Rise," said the father. "I rise," said the one.
So they rose from the ashes in the glimmer of the sun.

Over in the Woodland, where the stream runs blue,
Lived a mother unicorn and her unicorns two.

"Prance," said the mother. "We prance," said the two.
So they pranced and they played where the stream runs blue.

Over in the Woodland, where the lava meets the sea,
Lived a strong father cyclops and his cyclops children three.

"Forge," said the father. "We forge," said the three.
So they forged magic weapons where the lava meets the sea.

Over in the Woodland, where the waterfalls roar,
Lived a fair mother mermaid and her little mermaids four.

"Swim," said the mother. "We swim," said the four.
So they swam and they sang where the waterfalls roar.

Over in the Woodland, where the mountains come alive,
Lived a wise father dwarf and his little dwarves five.

"Carve," said the father. "We carve," said the five.
So they carved and they crafted where the mountains come alive.

Over in the Woodland, in the sky playing tricks,
Lived a fierce father dragon and his little dragons six.

"Fly," said the father. "We fly," said the six.
So they flew and they flamed in the sky playing tricks.

Over in the Woodland, in a lush, leafy heaven,
Lived a spry mother fairy and her little fairies seven.

"Dance," said the mother. "We dance," said the seven.
So they danced all around in a lush, leafy heaven.

Over in the Woodland, underneath a bridge of slate,
Lived a craggy mother troll and her little trolls eight.

"Climb," said the mother. "We climb," said the eight.
So they climbed and they crawled underneath a bridge of slate.

Over in the Woodland, near a tall, stately pine,
Lived a bold father centaur and his centaur foals nine.

"Aim," said the father. "We aim," said the nine.
So they aimed all their arrows near a tall, stately pine.

Over in the Woodland, in the quiet of their den,
Called the noble mother griffin to her little griffins ten.

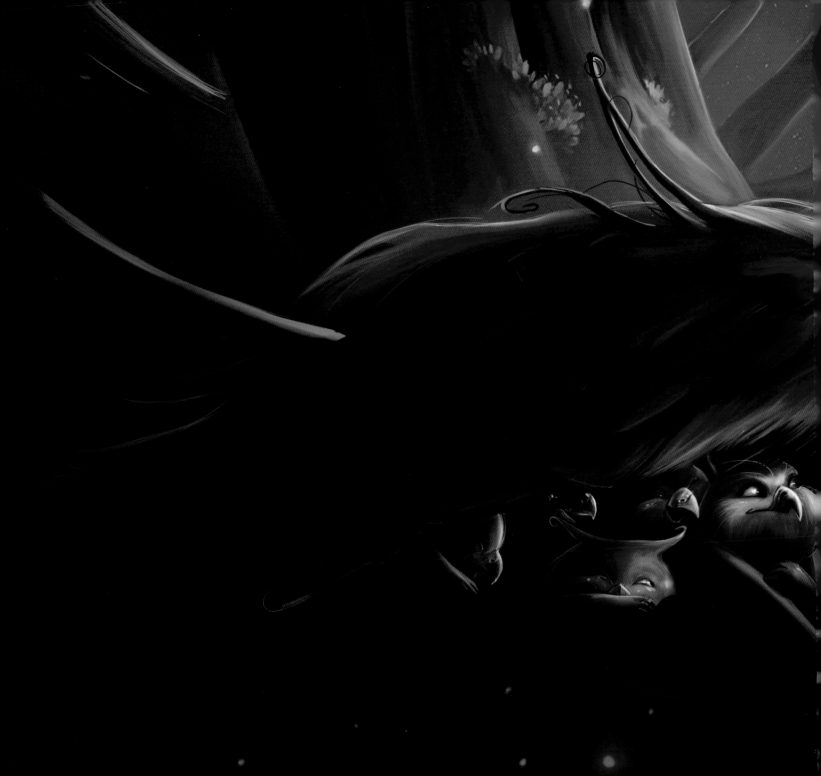

"Safe?" asked the mother. "All safe," said the ten.
So they settled for the night in the quiet of their den.

PHOENIX

A phoenix is a golden-red bird that is immortal. Every day, the phoenix builds a nest in the top of a tree using fine spices and fragrant woods, and every evening, it sings an exceptionally beautiful song as the sun sets the nest aflame. Then, the phoenix is consumed by the fire, but it is not destroyed. Each morning it is reborn, rising from the ashes as a new, powerful phoenix.

UNICORN

A unicorn is a glowing white horse with a pointed spiral horn in the middle of its forehead. A unicorn's horn has the power to heal. Unicorns are gentle and kind, but they will fight fiercely to avoid capture. They live in forests and are very hard to find, as they like to keep hidden.

CYCLOPS

A cyclops is an incredibly strong, one-eyed giant. Cyclopes are skilled blacksmiths who create weapons for the gods. They work in an underground forge next to a river of lava. Over time, their work underground caused volcanoes to form.

MERMAID

A mermaid is a water creature that has the upper body of a woman and the tail of a fish. Mermaids are enchanted beings who are kind but very shy. They avoid humans as much as possible, but they will help if someone is in trouble. They live in oceans and lakes and sing beautiful songs.

DWARF

A dwarf is a small, human-like being with magical powers. Dwarves live beneath mountains in underground caves. They are master craftsmen who carve and sculpt extraordinary treasures out of metal, wood, stone, and gems. Because of this talent, gods and other creatures come to dwarves when they need a special object created or repaired.

Dragon

A dragon is a large reptile with wings, a scaly body, and enormous claws and teeth. Like most reptiles, they lay eggs. Unlike most reptiles, they can spew fire and fly. Dragons desire fine gold and jewels, which they store in their lairs and guard ferociously. They live in mountains and caves and have extremely long lives.

Fairy

A fairy is a supernatural being with magical powers. Fairies look similar to humans but are tiny and have wings. They use their magic to interfere with humans, sometimes to help them, but often to be mischievous. However, no matter what trouble they might cause, fairies will always tell the truth. They love nature and work hard to protect the lush, green woods of their home.

Troll

A troll is a foul creature known for its great strength and dislike of humans. Trolls dwell in caves or under bridges. They only go out at night because they will turn to stone if sunlight touches their skin. Trolls live in family groups that consist of a father with daughters or a mother with sons.

Centaur

A centaur has the head, arms, and chest of a human and the body and legs of a horse. Centaurs roam forests in family groups called tribes. They are wise teachers who are gifted in healing, stargazing, and mathematics. They are also valiant warriors who are skilled in archery.

Griffin

A griffin is a creature that combines two of the world's mightiest animals: the eagle (king of the birds) and the lion (king of the beasts). They have a feathery upper body, with the head, front legs, and wings of an eagle, and a furry lower body, with the back legs and tail of a lion. Known for their courage and intelligence, griffins are guardians of treasure and protectors from evil.